Hail to Spring!

by
Charles Ghigna

raintree
a Capstone company — publishers for children

Springtime lightning flashes, soars.

Springtime thunder rumbles, roars.

Storms bring hail that falls like rain ...

rapping, tapping on the pane.

Balls of hail fall on the trees ...

dashing, crashing through the leaves.

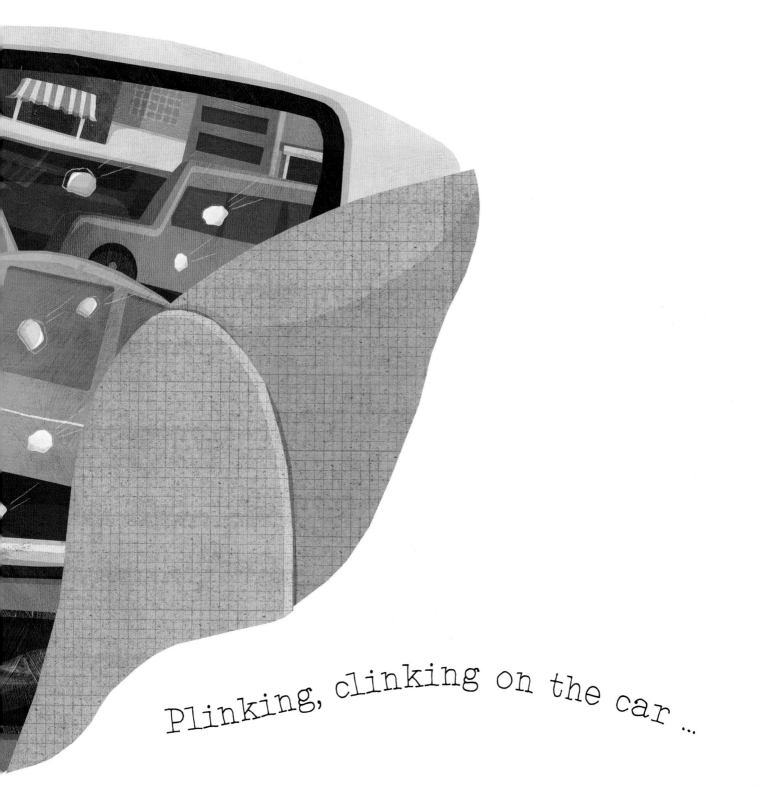

Plinking, clinking on the car ...

hail is falling near and far.

Shimmering, glimmering in the street ...

hail is dancing at our feet.

Sunshine melts the hail away.
We all run outside to play!

Time to laugh. Time to sing.
Time to say, "Hail to spring!"

All about hail

- Hail is a solid form of precipitation. Precipitation is rain, snow, sleet or hail that falls to the ground from clouds.

- Hail forms in cumulonimbus clouds. Cumulonimbus clouds produce thunderstorms.

- Hail freezes while it is in a cloud. Once the ball of ice falls to the ground, it is called a hailstone. Hailstones can be as small as a pea or as large as a tennis ball.

- Hailstorms can be dangerous. During a storm, stay indoors.

Cumulonimbus Cloud

anvil top

dark base

Titles in this series:

Hail to Spring!
Raindrops Fall All Around
Sunshine Brightens Springtime
A Windy Day in Spring

Websites

www.metoffice.gov.uk/education/kids

Explore the fascinating world of weather through games,
experiments, facts and photographs on the Met Office's
"For Kids" section of this interactive website.

For Charlotte and Christopher.

Thanks to our adviser for his expertise, research and advice:
Terry Flaherty, PhD, Professor of English

Raintree is an imprint of Capstone Global Library Limited, a company
incorporated in England and Wales having its registered office at 7
Pilgrim Street, London, EC4V 6LB – Registered company number: 6695582

www.raintree.co.uk
myorders@raintree.co.uk

Text © Capstone Global Library Limited 2015
The moral rights of the proprietor have been asserted.

Editorial Credits
Shelly Lyons and Elizabeth R. Johnson, editors; Lori Bye, designer; Nathan
Gassman, art director; Tori Abraham, production specialist

ISBN 978 1 4062 8864 3 (hardback)
18 17 16 15 14
10 9 8 7 6 5 4 3 2 1

ISBN 978 1 4062 8869 8 (paperback)
19 18 17 16 15
10 9 8 7 6 5 4 3 2 1

British Library Cataloguing in Publication Data
A full catalogue record for this book is available from the British Library.

Design Elements
The illustrations in this book were created with acrylics and digital
collage; Shutterstock: R2D2

Every effort has been made to contact copyright holders of material
reproduced in this book. Any omissions will be rectified in subsequent
printings if notice is given to the publisher.

All the Internet addresses (URLs) given in this book were valid at the time
of going to press. However, due to the dynamic nature of the Internet, some
addresses may have changed, or sites may have changed or ceased to exist
since publication. While the author and publisher regret any inconvenience
this may cause readers, no responsibility for any such changes can be
accepted by either the author or the publisher.

Printed and bound in China.